W9-BAH-718

MY DAD, MY HERO

BY ETHAN LONG

sourcebooks
jabberwocky

Copyright © 2011 by Ethan Long
Cover and internal illustrations © Ethan Long
Cover and internal design © 2011 by Sourcebooks, Inc.
Sourcebooks and the colophon are registered trademarks of Sourcebooks, Inc.

All rights reserved. No part of this book may be reproduced in any form or by any electronic or mechanical means including information storage and retrieval systems—except in the case of brief quotations embodied in critical articles or reviews—without permission in writing from its publisher, Sourcebooks, Inc.

The characters and events portrayed in this book are fictitious or are used fictitiously. Any similarity to real persons, living or dead, is purely coincidental and not intended by the author.

Published by Sourcebooks Jabberwocky, an imprint of Sourcebooks, Inc.
P.O. Box 4410, Naperville, Illinois 60567-4410
(630) 961-3900
Fax: (630) 961-2168
www.jabberwockykids.com

Library of Congress Cataloging-in-Publication data is on file with the publisher.

Source of Production: Leo Paper, Heshan City, Guangdong Province, China
Date of Production: January 2011
Run Number: 14148
Ages 4 and up

Printed and bound in China.
LEO 10 9 8 7 6 5 4 3 2 1

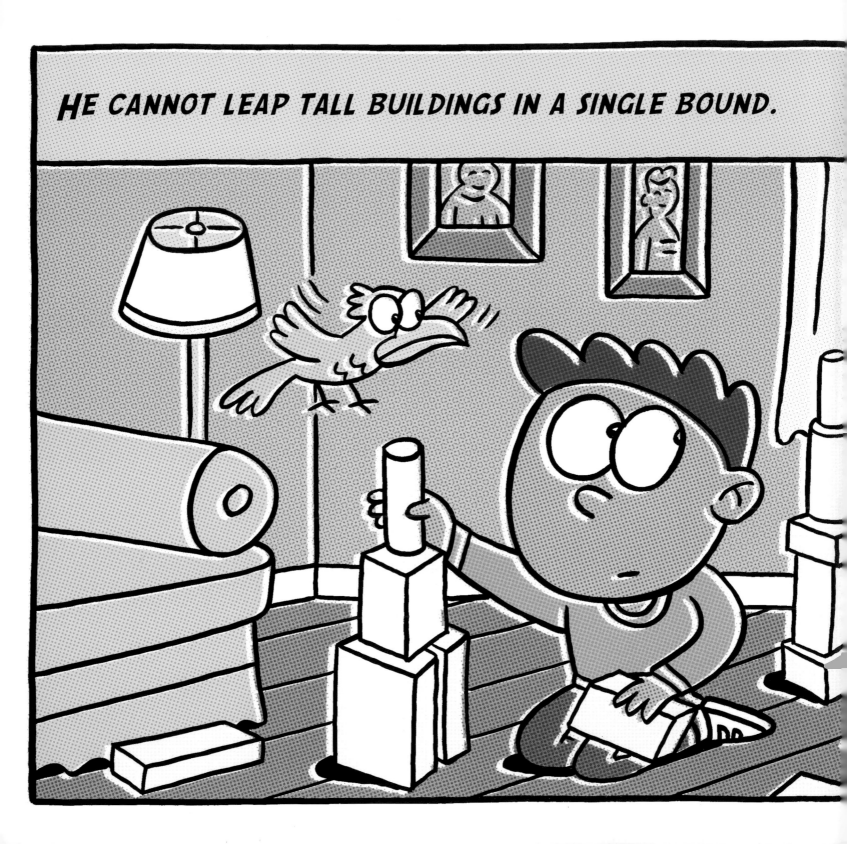

HE CANNOT LEAP TALL BUILDINGS IN A SINGLE BOUND.

MY DAD DOES SPEND A LOT OF TIME WITH ME.